BEAR LIBRARY
101 GOVERNOR'S PLACE
BEAR, DELAWARE 19701

W9-BRN-185

NObODY NOTiCES MiNERVA

by Wednesday Kirwan

STERLING

New York / London

STERLING and the distinctive Sterling logo are registered trademarks of
Sterling Publishing Co., Inc.

Library of Congress Cataloging-in-Publication Data
Kirwan, Wednesday.
Nobody notices Minerva / Wednesday Kirwan.
p. cm.
Summary: When Minerva wakes up in a bad mood and nobody notices,
she spends an entire day behaving badly—
until some loving advice from Dad helps turn things around.
ISBN-13: 978-1-4027-4728-1 ISBN-10: 1-4027-4728-4
[1. Behavior—Fiction. 2. Family life—Fiction.
3. Boston terrier—Fiction. 4. Dogs—Fiction.] I. Title.

PZ7.K6397Nob 2007
[E]—dc22
2006032921

2 4 6 8 10 9 7 5 3

Published by Sterling Publishing Co., Inc.
387 Park Avenue South, New York, NY 10016
www.SterlingPublishing.com/kids
Text and illustrations copyright © 2007 by Wednesday Kirwan
The artwork was prepared using gouache and colored pencils.
Designed by Lauren Rille

Distributed in Canada by Sterling Publishing
C/o Canadian Manda Group, 165 Dufferin Street, Toronto, Ontario, Canada M6K 3H6
Distributed in the United Kingdom by GMC Distribution Services,
Castle Place, 166 High Street, Lewes, East Sussex, England BN7 1XU
Distributed in Australia by Capricorn Link (Australia)
Pty. Ltd. P.O. Box 704, Windsor, NSW 2756, Australia

Printed in China
All rights reserved

Sterling ISBN-13: 978-1-4027-4728-1
ISBN-10: 1-4027-4728-4

For information about custom editions, special sales, premium and corporate purchases,
please contact Sterling Special Sales Department at 800-805-5489 or specialsales@sterlingpub.com.

TO MY DAD,
who always noticed

MINERVA woke up in a terrible mood. She had overslept, and nobody noticed.

When Minerva came down to breakfast,
Dad didn't notice.

"Open up for the oatmeal train," he told baby Keely.

Minerva sat down on the floor with her brother Francis and Mom, but they didn't notice.

"Try adding eight plus two," Mom said to Francis.

"Nobody ever notices me," grumbled Minerva.

So Minerva pulled out the stuffing
from the armrest in Dad's favorite chair.

She picked the leaves off Mom's plant with her toes.

She peeled up strips of wallpaper in the hallway.

And watched cartoons upside down.

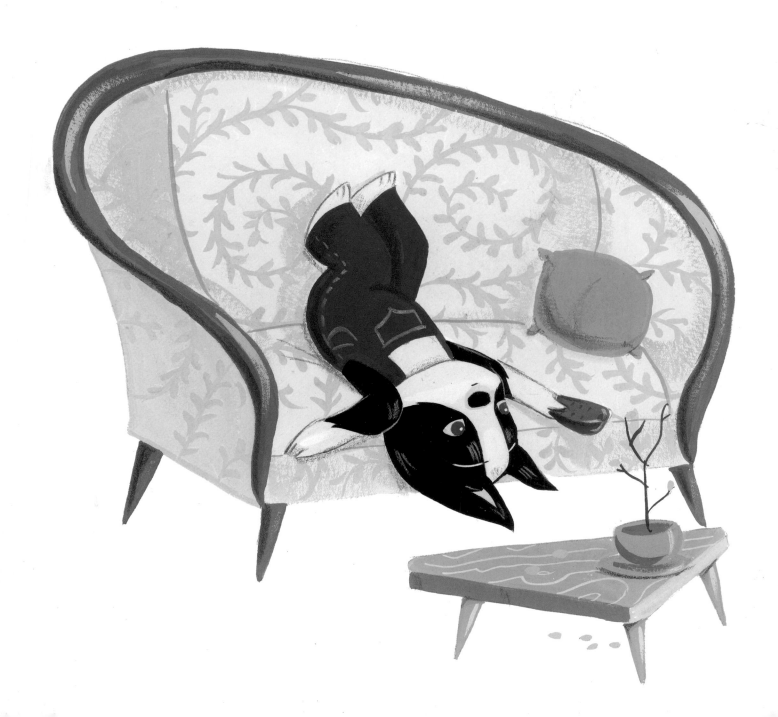

But nobody seemed to notice.

At lunch, Minerva knocked over an entire glass of milk.

She poked Francis with her fork, and stuck out her tongue at Keely.

After lunch, Minerva wrote the letter "m" on the door with a piece of chalk.

And kicked Francis's favorite *toy*

down

the

stairs.

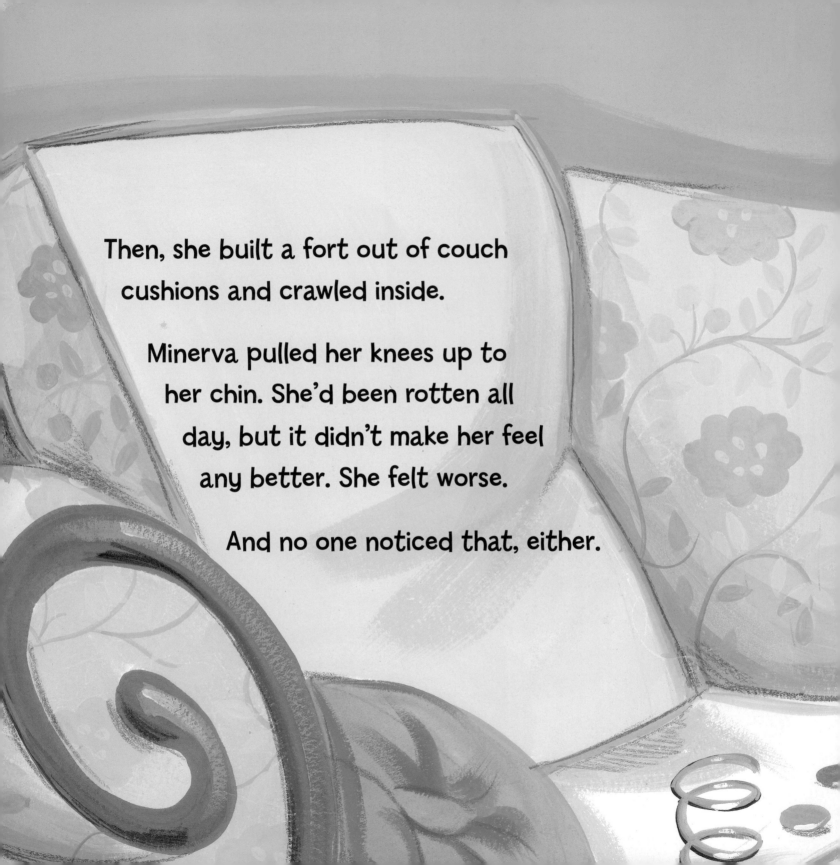

Then, she built a fort out of couch cushions and crawled inside.

Minerva pulled her knees up to her chin. She'd been rotten all day, but it didn't make her feel any better. She felt worse.

And no one noticed that, either.

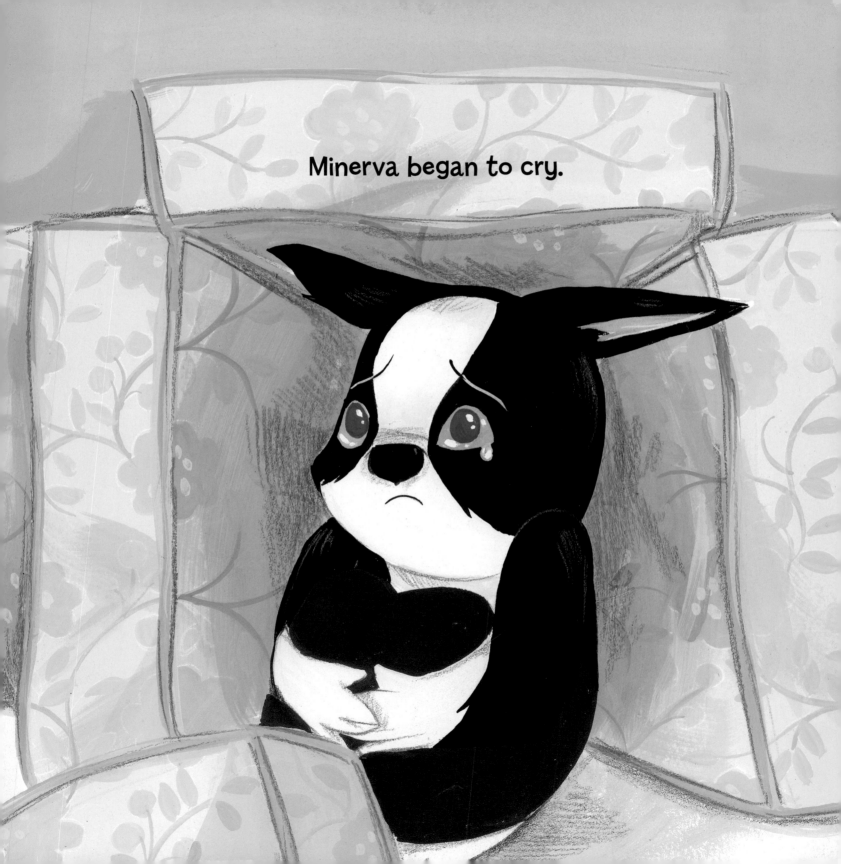

Minerva began to cry.

Dad heard her and sat down on
the other end of the couch.
"Minerva," Dad said softly,
"I *always* notice you.
You are my little firecracker.

Life is more exciting with you around.

But maybe it is better to be noticed for other things."

Dad squeezed Minerva's paw
through the wall of sofa cushions.
Minerva squeezed back.

She stopped crying and thought hard.

After a while, she crawled out from
under the sofa cushions and put them back.

She helped Mom sort the laundry and paired up all the socks.

She helped Francis set
the table without being asked.

And she read her favorite book to Keely.

Dad tucked Minerva in.
He said, "Hey there, my little potato.
I guess we'll keep you after all."

He winked at her.

Minerva smiled.

It was nice to be noticed.
She decided that from now on
she would be good *all* the time.

Starting tomorrow.

BEAR LIBRARY
101 GOVERNOR'S PLACE
BEAR, DELAWARE 19701

JE CDBK KIR
Kirwan, Wednesday.
Nobody notices Minerva
33910037072015   be
$37.75   05/28/08